God bless our sweet new baby
and may I always be
the kindest little helper
a blessing Lord for Thee.
                 Amen

The New Baby

by
Patricia Richardson Mattozzi

Published by The C.R. Gibson Company, Norwalk, CT 06856

Published by The C.R. Gibson Company
Norwalk, Connecticut 06856
Printed in the U.S.A.

GB388   ISBN 0-8378-7689-3

There's a new baby at my house
and everyone's really glad—
all our friends and neighbors
especially Mom and Dad!

Babies are so little
and the world is so wide,
— they need baby-sitters —
to stay close by their side.

We must be very careful
not to make a peep,
because little babies
must get lots of sleep.

Babies need attention;
they cry instead of talk.
Their diapers need changing
and they don't know how to walk.

Sometimes I feel forgotten
as people come to see
— the tiny new baby... —
did they forget about me?

Mom says it is a busy time
with the new baby here;
but we're all a great big family
each one is very dear.

I was a baby once,
and look—you were too!

Our Mom and Dad were happy
to take care of me and you.

Mom says she really loves me,
and that I should know,

as our family keeps getting bigger
her love for us will grow.

Our parents' love is something
all of us must share,

And I can help my parents
by giving all my loving care.

God loves our whole family
each sister and each brother.
We are all God's children,
so we love one another!

How great is the love the Father has lavished on us,
that we should be called children of God!

I John 3:1